I will be thin and pure like a glass cup. I move my hands over my body — my shoulders, collar bone, my rib cage, my hip bones like part of an animal skull, my small thighs. In the mirror my face is pale and my eyes look bruised.

In a house on a hill below the Hollywood sign there was hurt and blades and breaking glass. There was pain and shards and sharpness. Until Laurel's father died and she was left with emptiness. Now all Laurel needs to do is heal.

Also by Francesca Lia Block

Weetzie Bat
Witch Baby
Cherokee Bat and the Goat Guys
Missing Angel Juan
Baby Be-Bop
Girl Goddess #9: *Nine Stories*
Dangerous Angels: *The Weetzie Bat Books*
I Was a Teenage Fairy
Violet & Claire
The Rose and The Beast
Echo
Guarding the Moon
Wasteland

The Hanged Man

Francesca Lia Block

Joanna Cotler Books
HarperCollins*Publishers*

The Hanged Man
Copyright © 1994 by Francesca Lia Block
All rights reserved. No part of this book may be used or reproduced in any manner whatsoever without written permission except in the case of brief quotations embodied in critical articles and reviews. Printed in the United States of America. For information address HarperCollins Publishers, 10 East 53rd Street, New York, NY 10022.

Library of Congress Cataloging-in-Publication Data
Block, Francesca Lia.
　The Hanged Man / Francesca Lia Block.
　　p.　　cm.
　Includes bibliographical references.
　Summary: Having stopped eating after the death of her father, seventeen-year-old Laurel feels herself losing control of her life in the hot, magical world of Los Angeles.
　ISBN 0-06-024536-0. — ISBN 0-06-024537-9 (lib. bdg.)
　ISBN 0-06-440832-9 (pbk.)
　[1. Death—Fiction. 2. Emotional problems—Fiction. 3. Anorexia nervosa—Fiction. 4. Los Angeles (Calif.)—Fiction. 5. Fathers and daughters—Fiction. 6. Incest—Fiction.]　I. Title.
PZ7.B61945Han　1994　　　　　　　　　　　　　　　94-720
[Fic]—dc20　　　　　　　　　　　　　　　　　　　CIP
　　　　　　　　　　　　　　　　　　　　　　　AC

Typography by Steven M. Scott
First paperback edition, 1999
❖
www.harpercollins.com

For my parents,
who gave me courage to explore
the darkest parts of my imagination

The Hanged Man

THE MOON.

"Turn up the First Card; cover the Significator therewith, and say: That covers him. This is the person or thing's general environment at the time, the influence with which he is actuated all through."

1. The Moon

At first I think he looks like a skull, like he is wearing a skull mask. Because somehow the dark glasses look concave like sockets and his face is so thin and white. I think about the skulls they paint in Mexico for the Day of the Dead—little skulls and dangling, dancing skeletons everywhere. He is junky-thin but still bulky around the shoulders and arms, muscley, the way the muscles stay intact after the junk's worn away at the flesh. And he is wonderfully white in the fluorescence of the hospital waiting room.

He looks up from his book and nods at me. Then he says hello and his voice is the best thing—it cracks like ice when you pour the liquor over.

"You've been here a long time," he says. I guess it's easy to tell I haven't slept—my clothes are wrinkled and I can feel the shadowy cloud pressing around my eyes.

"I've lost count."

"Why're you here?"

"My father."

I think of my father in the room down the hall—what is supposed to still be my father. Gaping, hooked up with tubes. My mother still not believing, still speaking to him, pleading. As if that was still him. When I look at what is supposed to still be him, I can't remember anything. The way his eyes are the color of the bronze women he made when he was young. The way he used to take splinters out of my hands. Make pancakes shaped like animals. Press his mouth against me, warming my skin with his breath.

"I hate this waiting. Here. It feels sick. You start wishing it would be over with," I say.

"You probably need a break," the man says. "To drive to the beach. Get some air at least."

I notice that his lips are full, different from the rest of his face.

Maybe it is his voice. Or that hospitals are supposed to make people horny. Or that it's the biggest rebound of my life with my father in there dying. But I wish this man would come over to me and press his mouth to my mouth and hold the balls of my shoulders, hold them as if he could crush them to splinters in his hands.

"I better get back," I say, standing up.

"What's your name?"

I tell him Laurel and he says, "Jack."

"I'll see you, Laurel," he says and his voice is full in his throat as if he has said something else, something more.

I go down the hall that is quiet except for a

cough and these liquid sounds. My mother is standing outside of my father's room with her face in her hands. The doctor is saying something to her.

My mother feels like a marionette made of string and wood as I lead her out of the hospital and into the heat.

There are black birds hunched in the oleander bushes. As we drive home, we pull up next to a truck with metal bars. Inside, something roars, some caged thing pacing, lashing its tail.

We drive up the canyon under the Hollywood sign. It used to say Hollywoodland like Alice in Wonder or Disney but now it just says Hollywood as in wood of hollys. Or Holy Wood. I think people have tried to leap off of it and die, or is that just in books?

Below the canyon stretches out like an umbilical cord to the belly of the city and up we go past the Spanish-style apartments where the girl got raped last week, some man prowling outside her pink stucco walls while she lay on her bed. Broke the glass. Past the canyon market where I worked last summer, packing bags full of yogurts, avocados, peaches, and wine for the canyon people—the long-haired, junky musicians from My Animal and Shocks and Struts, the beautiful lesbian models Rebecca and Sophie, shaved punk kids, artists in paint-spattered clothes and bone jewelry, film types in cowboy boots and jeans carrying scripts. Past the cafe —they all hang out there too—where Claudia and I drink coffee (mine black, hers sugary and milky brown) and smoke at the window booth with the sun dusting in like some kind of drug we want to put in our noses and mouths and veins.

And up where it winds toward the crest of the hill, past the old stone castles, Spanish villas, Moroccan palaces, gabled fairy-tale cottages— all built for movie stars a long time ago. Charlie Chaplin's house that was a fancy whorehouse after that. And the house where Victoria and her daughter, Perdita, and Victoria's various boyfriends all live. It's covered with hibiscus in front and the blue glass windows must make Perdita feel like she is in some kind of a fish tank.

Tucked in the hills is the lake where the runners circle, passing the rusty metal tubing I have nightmares about, going over the bridge with the carved lion heads and the water below getting sucked down into a whirlpool drain.

At the top of the canyon are our two houses—Claudia and her mother, Eva's palace and our house. Both of them under the Hollywood sign looking down over the stretch of canyon to the mother belly city like children attached to an old cord.

We live in a house with a tower. The man who built it was a toymaker; he carved the faces over the fireplace and planted the vines that cover the walls and the oleander in the garden. It smells like cedar and eucalyptus, smoke and lavender in this house. There are things everywhere: books, shells, fossils, dried flowers, bird skulls, the antique wooden cherub, the miniature stone sphinx, ivory monkeys, the brass menorah, china dolls with little teeth, the ancient Roman tear vessel that came from a tomb—that looks like a fossilized tear itself; the three bronze women stand erect. My father made them before I was born.

I go into the kitchen and put some plums and a slice of buttered, home-baked bread onto a blue-and-white plate from Holland. I fill a glass with water and squeeze some lemon in. I put everything on the tray with the real butterflies pressed under glass. Then I bring it in to my mother. She is sitting on the green velvet chair that still has cat hair on it, holding her sides, her arms crisscross. I leave the tray beside her and go to call everybody, thinking it will be easier to just get it over with. People are crying and saying O My God O My God and I have to comfort them, especially the older ones whose voices vibrate with the thought of their own deaths. I have to say, he wasn't in too much pain . . . it was sudden . . . no, it was less painful than they expected. I go through the red leather book name by name, but not really thinking. I don't know half of these people and the ones I do know seem to blur together. I'm happy when I get an answering machine. Beep. My father died. I feel like a machine too—my jaw a steel trapdoor.

After the last call I hang up and listen. It seems quieter in our house now. Why is it so quiet? Nothing is rattling in the cupboards, no sound of trembling glass and china. I know that nothing will break anymore.

Three pink wineglasses. The china mermaid bell. My father's reading glasses. An ivory hand mirror. Nine blue-and-white plates from Holland. On and on. My mother kept a list. She told me, "This has got to stop. We will have to eat off the table." I said, "It's not me." But once I threw an empty wine bottle to the floor as hard as I could. It broke into green pieces. They were like the cold, hard, gritty fragments I imagine lodged in my throat sometimes. I wanted to know what it felt like to break something—with my hands instead.

I know that nothing will break anymore. Not the way things used to break. Clattering, crashing, smashing, shattering by themselves. It is very quiet in our house now.

I lie awake in my bed in the tower room, my cigarette becoming ash. The moon looks too big, swollen like a belly full of blood. My period doesn't come and the moon swells more each month. I touch myself furiously, trying to set the blood free. I'm not pregnant; the doctor says it's because I don't eat. My bones feel starved, chalky. The moon, resentful that she can't make me bleed, pulls and pulls on my belly and my swollen heart, saying, if you won't bleed I'll drag at your very bones.

My mother says, "I am a Gypsy witch. I am a Gypsy witch."

She laughs. "Today in the market, a little girl pointed at me and said to her mother, 'Mommy, see the witch!' The mother was embarrassed and said, 'Oh, a lot of ladies wear black dresses!' I started to laugh," my mother says.

Her hair is long and pulled back severely and she wears pointed black boots and silver charms. But it mostly has to do with her eyes.

My mother walks around holding the peonies I bought her as if they were children—cradling the petally heads in her arms. She says, "I saw another white moth today. They follow me everywhere. Every time I leave the house." I have seen them whitening the air around her head like her thoughts flying. I think she thinks they are my father's spirit. I say, "Maybe you shouldn't talk so much about those moths in front of other people."

My mother is cleaning in a frenzy—spraying, wiping, scrubbing, dusting, boiling, bleaching. My mother is cooking and cooking. She buys turkeys and reaches inside of them and takes out what is there and rubs the flesh all over with garlic and stuffs them with vegetables and bakes them in the oven. It has been hot and the kitchen feels like an oven. I feel like those children that the witch stuffed into an oven in the fairy tale. The kitchen smells of garlic and animal and yeast from the breads my mother bakes. My mother bakes breads and she makes them in the shapes of women with breasts, of mermaids with braids, of fat animals, and moons with faces. Sometimes she doesn't sleep; she stays up all night cooking and she won't listen to me when I tell her to sleep. She says, "Come in here and eat something, you're too skinny. I think you have that disease. What is that disease called? The one where those girls stop eating." I feel like Hansel and Gretel. Didn't the witch stuff them in an oven?

But I won't eat all that candy Hansel and Gretel ate. I will be thin and pure like a glass cup. Empty. Pure as light. Music. I move my hands over my body—my shoulders, collar bone, my rib cage, my hipbones like part of an animal skull, my small thighs. In the mirror my face is pale and my eyes look bruised. My hair is pale and thin and the light comes through. I could be a lot younger than seventeen. I could be a child still, untouched.

I used to just be afraid of getting pregnant and V.D. and getting hurt, of the way I'd feel transparent afterward as if my skin showed the man I was with everything underneath. That he could see my organs and my bones. Now they've started saying on the news how sex can kill you.

Dying from needles and love. It's like a nightmare demon coming in through bedroom windows. It's like the devil came the first time, breaking in a window with a body of wounds and syringes full of poison blood.

On the news they said there is some killer in the hills who's been breaking in through windows at night and raping women and cutting their throats so I lock my windows but I don't sleep well now. When I do sleep, I have all these dreams. Mostly, I dream about a man.

In one dream I see him stand, I don't see his face but I recognize him. And he takes off this blue kimono that slides over the shadow of bare shoulders like it's silk and the shoulders are very smooth. It is so real. I can feel the way the cold silk has absorbed the heat of his skin.

In a dream he is in one of those old five-and-dimes looking through bins of weird things in the dark—miniature plates and chairs and colored glass beads and plastic flowers. He has these huge green, red, and yellow parrots perched on his shoulders and they have big, sharp beaks and eyes like beads. They make terrible sounds. I am afraid they will fly in my face with beaks and claws and feathers. Desire is a parrot. When I was little, my mother would leave me in my room with Zack. He would be out of his cage, sitting there cleaning his feet and staring at me with one eye.

Once, I dreamed the man was standing among the oleanders, eating the flowers and smiling so his teeth showed. They grow in front of our house—oleanders. My mother said, "They're poisonous, Laurel." The flowers look like cigarette cherries. I used to wonder if you'd die right away from eating the flowers. We had a white cat named Sugar that used to play in the bushes and I would try to catch her because I was afraid she would die from eating the flowers.

It isn't just dreams though. I was taking a shower one night and the door was closed. I always lock my doors. Slipping soapy fingers over my body, it was like someone was there, like someone was touching me. And when I got out of the shower, the door was open.

Last night, I dreamed he was made of gold and he touched me and made me gold too. He looked wonderful with the muscles in his neck and arms gleaming. But I wanted him to touch me inside too so that I would be gold inside and not feel things.

Remember the story about King Midas? He touched everything and made it gold. Including his daughter and then he had her forever and ever. Finally, he starved to death because the food he touched turned gold. My father told me that story. He stroked my hair and he said I had hair like Midas's daughter and wasn't he lucky that he had a gold child like King Midas? And what if my whole body were gold like that?

This morning, Claudia said, "You need some sun. Look at you. You look gray. You need to get your blood moving."

At the Venice boardwalk it is hot but the sun is bandaged in clouds. Claudia and I rent roller skates and roll through — bodies all around us. We see the skating veiled man with pale eyes who makes electronic sounds from his throat, not just his guitar. And the seaweed man. The muscle men heaving metal behind a chain-link fence. The mermaid woman with blond hair to her waist and the long mermaid body streaming by on skates. There is a man who breaks liquor bottles and jumps off a chair onto the jagged pieces. Some people from the audience stand on his chest. At first everyone laughs but pretty soon their expressions change. I pull Claudia away.

Claudia buys a piece of pizza. The rich smell of scalding cheese. "You should eat," she says. But I don't take a bite. I'm smoking, inhaling hard.

The clown is a tiny man in whiteface who sits on the boardwalk painting people. He asks me,

"What do you dream about?" and I tell him about the parrots and the poison flowers and the gold. So he paints delicately while I speak, tracing the brush like a tongue over my forehead and cheeks and eyelids. He paints me my dreams but I can't see them. I feel my dreams being licked onto my face with paint. Then he holds up the mirror. I see feathers and blossoms — scarlet highlighted with gold.

The clown paints Claudia's dreams on her face. He paints crescent moons and pomegranates and crosses. He paints her pale blue and silver.

"We are beautiful," Claudia says when he is through. "There's a party in Laurel Canyon," she says.

At the party in the canyon I was named for, everyone is sweating in the heat in the rooms with low ceilings, masks on the walls. The air smells like burned meat. These little kids are running around barefoot with their hair in their faces; their feet are really dirty and they are screaming and waving sticks with pieces of colored paper tied on. Perdita, who is six and a half, is leading them. She has flowers in her hair—those blue ones that stick by themselves and wilt in the heat.

Shane's hair is freshly dyed blue. Paradise is spinning around and around in her circus petticoat. Her eyes like pinwheels. She says, "I haven't slept for days. Meredith's been away." Meredith is Tommy's girlfriend but Paradise sleeps with Tommy when Meredith is out of town. Perdita's mother, Victoria, is wearing one of the masks and drinking through the mask mouth with a straw. Some man is kissing her neck. Claudia goes to get a drink. I don't want her to leave me.

This weasel guy comes up and puts his arms around me, his fingers just brushing under my breasts where I am soaked with sweat. He says,

"I got some coke." I'm trying to pull away when I see that man from the hospital. Jack.

"Jack."

He's wearing a shirt woven with Guatemalan snake feather ghost patterns in bright colors. He tells the weasel to leave and the weasel lets go of me and walks away. He says, "I knew I'd see you again. How are you?"

I am drinking something right out of the bottle and the paint on my face is running in the heat so everything looks streaky blue. This summer is already so hot that you wake up sweating and your makeup runs before you even leave the house.

"Okay. Mostly okay." I put my hand to my temples as if the dizziness will stop that way.

And he says, "Come with me," like you would say come to a lover, come not follow, and we walk out of the low rooms and down the dirt path, down the hill from the party and across the canyon road—we have to run across because the cars go fast here and it's hard for me to run in my heels and he grabs my wrist.

Across the canyon are the ruins of the castle, just some ruins, some crumbling stone among the weeds. My father used to drive me here when I was little and tell me how Houdini lived here once. And wouldn't I like to stop and see if we could find something, something magical that the magician possessed?

Jack leads me up the hill among the ruins and I think maybe he is humming but I'm not sure—maybe it is just the heat.

It smells of eucalyptus and smoke. It is hot and I feel mosquitos sucking my arms.

"Welcome to Houdini's palace," Jack says in a voice you would use to help a child fall asleep. "This is the hallway . . . and here is the dining room. Houdini's cook has served some broiled rabbit, champagne, cake and ice cream. Pistachio. Served in top hats." We walk up onto a raised area of the foundation. "The game room.

But you'll never win. The cards float right out of your hands here. Be careful of the rabbits running around. . . . A flower?" He pulls a wild rose off its stem. "But be careful," he says, tucking it into my blouse between my breasts. "It might change into a garden or some animal. And, of course, the bedroom." He leads me over some broken stone. "The bed with the straps. Houdini liked to challenge his escapist powers, even in his sleep. Sometimes he slept suspended upside down too. But we'll lie down the regular way I think."

He unbuttons his shirt and takes it off. His body is smooth and defined.

"Is this okay?" he asks, his voice suddenly even softer as he lays the shirt out on the dry grass. "Are you scared?"

"Yes. But I want to be here."

He sits down and takes my hand, pulling me down beside him. Then he kisses my cheek, my neck. I turn up my face to him and he kisses my mouth, catching my lower lip with his teeth the way you would a piece of fruit.

"I've wanted you since the hospital," he says. "You looked so little sitting there. I wanted to take you to the ocean. You look like you should be in water. Like a mermaid."

"No," I say. "No tail." I pull the antique silk skirt up above my knees.

I am so wet that when he touches me his hands slip down over my hipbones, my sunken belly and between my thighs. I feel something under me and arch up and reach around and find a ring. It is big and silver with two figures joined by a snake. Jack fingers it with one big hand. I notice that the veins in his hands are big with blood. He smiles and slips the ring onto my finger. I feel his body on top of me—his crushing shoulders, the ledge of his hips, his bruising thighs. I know I will be bruised tomorrow. Blood roses will bloom under my skin.

"Laurel," he says. "Is that really your name?

Like the canyon."

I think about the giants. I used to dream about giants all the time. They loomed over me and their thick fingers numbed me like cocaine and I couldn't breathe. But they were beautiful, my giants. Their eyes were like globes, blue-mapped-yellow, turning and turning in their heads.

"Laurel," he says.

I reach for his sunglasses but he tosses back his head and catches my wrist. He arches and parts his lips as if he is in pain. I watch his throat work above me in the twilight, working as if he has swallowed something live.

THE MAGICIAN.

"Turn up the Second Card; put it across him horizontally, and say: This is his obstacle."

II. The Magician

Every night I lie awake for hours kneading between my legs with my knuckles, the heat pressing and slipping on my body. When I finally fall asleep, I dream a lot, seeing pictures of that man Jack's face flickering on my brain in quick sequence like home movies on a screen. Jack Jack Jack. I dream we are in a palace with pink-veined marble walls and far-away ceilings. Some people are seated at a big table that is covered with wreaths of flowers and candles. They are feasting on animals and wines and liqueurs and flaming cakes and the woman at the head of the table wears a veil. Jack, in a Mad-Hatter oversized top hat, takes my hand. We roll down the pink hallways, as if our feet are roller skates, while bubbles turn to flowers to birds to stars in the air around us.

Cannon, who puts on all the big music shows, is having a party at his house in the hills. Blond boys drift around in the steam that comes up from the pool, in the greenish steam, and Perdita is swimming. You can hear the animals. They say Cannon keeps animals to get boys. It's something about being around that perfection that arouses people. Peacocks; there are parrots and monkeys and snakes. You can hear the tiger if you stand just at the edge of the music and the sound of glasses touching. Cannon keeps the tiger in a cage somewhere.

I see a handsome man—one of the best-looking men I have ever seen, even for Cannon's parties: sculptural, tan, broad-shouldered. But he is wearing sunglasses and smoking like crazy and his hand holding the cigarette is shaking so much he can hardly keep the cigarette between his fingers. He is walking with a cane and he is young, maybe in his thirties, and beautiful, still. You can tell everyone must have loved him, been helplessly in love with him. And you can tell how he's dying from something in his blood. He walks past with his cane and some boys stop laughing and look down into their drinks and no one says anything to him.

I turn and see Jack standing by the pool drinking from a bottle and wearing black jeans. The rest of him is naked. The lights reflecting off the water slide green moons all over his face and arms. He doesn't have sunglasses on and his eyes are deep-set and slanted.

Perdita swims to the edge of the pool and

climbs out near Jack. He wraps her in a towel tenderly and dries her hair which is green from the chlorine and the lights. Then he picks her up and carries her through a sliding glass door into the house.

He comes back and walks over to me.

"Laurel," he says, touching my hair the way you would touch really old lace or spiderwebs.

"How do you know Perdita?" I ask.

"Little Lost One it means. Lost childhood. I've known her for a long time," he says. "You look beautiful."

"Thanks. You look wild."

Cannon's tiger roars somewhere far away by the water. "My familiar," he says, laughing.

"Your familiar? Oh, you mean those witch animals. My mother has a parrot like that."

"Your mother's a witch?"

"I think she thinks so."

"How about you?"

"My father used to say, you should just learn how to use it. Not get all crazy and call it witchcraft. He said I should paint."

"That would be good for you probably."

The tiger roars again.

"When my father died, my mother and I left the hospital and saw this truck with some animal in it, right in the middle of the city, some animal roaring like that in the back of a truck. It was pretty weird. I kept thinking that was him. My father."

"Maybe," Jack says. His eyes look wet. "He's probably happier like that. I'd be happier in some animal."

"I need a drink," I say.

I go to the bar and when I look back to where we were standing, he is gone. So I walk to the edge of the lawn and listen. I can hear the water in the distance and the tiger again.

I take off my shoes and walk down among

the hibiscus and ivy where it is wet and dark. Palm trees are outlined against the greenish night sky like part of Cannon's menagerie.

And I see him, Jack, sitting by the creek that runs along the edge of Cannon's property. His head is down and there are shadows on his shoulders and spine like hands, like caresses.

I come up to him, close enough to touch him, and he turns around. His head looms, dark and toothy and wild and furred—the head of a bear on his pale body.

I have been wondering for a long time if I can still bleed. The doctor says it's because I don't eat. I feel like one of those people in a movie I saw on TV once with my father where all the people's blood dries up like chalk and sometimes I feel like that, like one of those bloodless people. Sometimes I think about that movie and I remember how my father said he wondered what kind of a mind made up a disease like that and I think that no one could have imagined a disease like the one now, the way people are dying now, dying as their blood mingles. But I want this man to show me my blood. I want him to make it run down my neck and the flesh along the insides of my arms. The teeth sinking into flesh, tearing flesh like wet silk.

I remember going downstairs to my father's study. It was like sleepwalking. My legs and arms felt heavy. My father was sitting at his desk marking his students' chemistry papers with a red pen.

My father looked up. Then he pointed to the Tarot cards scattered on the floor. "What are these doing here?"

I could not remember bringing the cards into his study. I wasn't allowed in there alone. I could not remember spilling the cards on the floor. But they don't do that by themselves. Like cups—cups don't break by themselves either.

I remember that I had dreamed of flying cards, cards like winged creatures. Flapping like the wings of frenzied moths. Whirring, stirring the air.

And where they had fallen—not in the dream, but really, where they had fallen, the Magician card lay on top. "The Magician—Skill, diplomacy, address; sickness, pain, loss, disaster; self-confidence, will" and reversed—"Physician, Magus, mental disease, disgrace, disquiet." He raises his arm above his head. His eyes are a blur.

"What is this?" my father said and his voice was like something breaking.

It says on my Tarot cards that this deck was originally drawn by a girl who grew up in Jamaica. We went to Jamaica once, my mother and my father and I. When we got off the boat, men came from everywhere and they whispered things to us, they whispered, "Doctor Man," and

"Something for your head," "Cure your ills," and the names of sweet things, strange, sweet things that I didn't understand then. My mother pulled me along and I remember she was wearing a red skirt with little mirrors sewn on it that she'd bought in one of those hippy stores she used to go to and the sunlight was splintering against the mirrors. My father's sunglasses were like mirrors too. He kept them on. He was talking to one of the men. I had never seen dreadlocks and I thought of snakes.

In Jamaica, there was a man named Doc with a van and he drove us through the hills. There was a dirt road winding around among all the green and the big flowers that looked like organs, like dripping hearts and lungs. I remember the flowers like that now. Then, I think I thought they were beautiful, like shells full of Jamaican sunsets.

Doc drove us to the top of a hill where there

was this inn but it was deserted. Except for this girl with the thinnest legs, bare feet and a rummy voice. She showed us around the inn. There was a pool with no water in it but painted pale blue and I looked down into the pale blue basin. There were hot rooms with reed mats on the floor and big, carved wooden beds. There was wild green around the place with goats and fruits, "pawpaws," the girl said, and a swing. My mother pushed me on the swing. My father stood looking out over the hills. He was smoking and his hands were shaking. The girl gave us ginger beers. Ginger beer burns your mouth and throat but it is dark and sweet.

When we drove down the roads in Jamaica, men would pop out from the bushes and stand in the road and make Doc stop the van. They came up to the windows of the van with handfuls of necklaces made of shell and seed pods or with carved wooden figures. They leaned into the van and their voices thickened around us like the heat in the air. My father kept his sunglasses on and he didn't look at them and he said to Doc, "Keep driving." Once, there was a man with a woven cage over his head. The cage was covered with vines and red flowers. The man's eyes were the same color as the flowers. "That's the Magic Man," Doc said. "Keep driving," my father said. The man in the road waved his hands mysteriously in front of his caged face and began to chant after us.

Once, there was a man in the road with two parrots on his shoulders. They were big and green with red chests. My mother called to them. They reminded her of Zack.

Along the road were little shacks with laundry strung on the lines and pigs running in the yards and thin, dark children. They stared at me. Doc took us to the falls.

My mother and I held hands and guides held

our other hands and helped us climb the falls. The water poured down to the blue sea. It wanted to pull us down with it. My feet slipped on the mossy rocks but the guide kept me from falling. I remember the curve of his arm, how his arms shone in the sun. I remember how his palms were paler than the rest of him and always seemed to stay dry, no matter how much water poured over us.

My father watched from the side, from the trees along the falls, while my mother and I climbed. He wore sunglasses and took photographs of us climbing the falls.

After, we ate barbecued chicken and black beans and fried bananas—plantain—in a little shack at the base of the falls.

There was a marketplace and the people came and gathered around us and started talking. Some of the women touched my hair and said, "Let us braid it, it's so white." They talked and talked. They all wanted us to buy. They had pink shells that looked like flowers and you could hear the falls in them, they said. They had carvings out of wood. I remember this huge head of a man with wooden snake hair and wooden jaguars and panthers and fish and birds. My mother bought lots of beads for gifts and she put them around her neck and wrapped them around and around her wrists. She bought some perfume called White Witch that smelled lemony and powdery. My father disappeared for a while and left us there and I couldn't find my mother either and my feet were bare because I had been swimming and the women touched my hair and said, "Let us braid it, it's so white." When my mother found me I was crying and she sprayed some White Witch on me and put some beads around my neck.

At night we slept at the inn. Bugs bit me and I was covered with welts turning chalky pink from the dried Caladryl lotion and I scratched my bitten, sunburned back on the rough cot and lay awake, my eyes, glazed from the heat, feeling like marbles in my head. Some nights I heard my mother and father through the walls. She gasped and gasped; her voice sounded far away. Sometimes I heard his voice biting back the words. I did not hear what he said but he sounded angry. I lay awake, afraid, reassured by my mother's gasps, also terrified of them.

One evening, while my mother was out marketing, my father came into my room. He lifted me up onto his feet and danced me around on his feet, around and around to the reggae music playing on his little radio. He looked especially pale and he kept wiping his nose and moving his shoulders. Maybe it was a reflection of bars of light from the window, but that was when I looked up and saw blades reflected in my father's eyes.

I look at my Tarot cards and try to think what the girl saw when she drew them. The colors are like Jamaica. There are green hills, blue skies, red, red flowers. But the people's skins — all of them — the High Priestess, Strength, the Star, the World — are white.

QUEEN of CUPS.

"This crowns him. It represents (a) the best that he can arrive at, or (b) his ideal in the matter; (c) what he wants to make his own; (d) but it is not his own at present."

III. The Queen of Cups

When I was little, I would go over to Claudia's to play. Claudia and her mother, Eva, live across the street in a palace, really—white with turrets and balconies and lacey windows. Inside, there are Moroccan archways, blue tiled floors, a reflecting pool with lilies, a tower overlooking the hills, the lake and the whole city. One Fourth of July, Claudia and I swayed on the balcony with the fireworks and the champagne in our heads exploding. The sky filled with crysanthemums and peacocks of fire like the sky was coming.

The house was built in the twenties by a film guy who gave wild parties, filled the reflecting pool with champagne, set off his own fireworks from the tower, filled the gardens with peacocks and lanterns. When Claudia's father, Jerome, bought it, it was a ruin—"rats in the walls, inches of ants like carpeting." Before Jerome decided to leave Eva, to live in South America with his twenty-two-year-old lover, Mayro, he had made the house beautiful again—painted, polished, exterminated. "The only thing he made beautiful, besides Claudia," Eva said. Already, in the five years since he's been gone, it has begun to fall apart again. Sometimes, Claudia and I hear rats in the walls.

Eva wanders around listening to the house. She has one blind, blue eye that rolls upward. She blinded herself, people say, to see. People come over to have her read their Tarot cards.

"When I was a kid," Claudia told me, "Eva

started to read my cards and when she saw them, she got all pale and goes, 'We'll do this some other time.' And I saw that Death card and some other really creepy-looking ones with swords and I thought, Oh great, she sees I'm going to get some horrible disease or something. And I always think about that. I mean, sometimes I feel like I fuck myself up because of it, you know?"

"That's why I hate them," I said. "Those cards. They're cool if you use them like symbols. I think you can learn from them. But I heard about this pregnant lady that went to a psychic who said the baby in her was this demon and to get rid of it and the lady freaked and did. That is really sick."

Claudia and I used to sneak into the secret room where Eva did her readings. It was a dim room filled with statues of human bodies with the heads of baboons and falcons and cats. They are really copies of the jars the Egyptians used for people's insides when they died. There was a black candle shaped like a skull, exactly the size and shape of one, as if someone had melted wax over a skull and stuck a wick on top.

My father had a story about a skull from when he was young and wanted to be an artist. He was living in Mexico and he got a skull from somewhere to sketch and sculpt. He was walking down the street in Mexico City and the skull fell out of the bag. It rolled on the sidewalk and people stopped and looked at this unshaven white guy, my father, as if he were a murderer, he used to say, and not an artist.

But Claudia and I came into the secret room mostly not for Eva's skull candle but to see her Tarot cards, even though they frightened us. They were very worn. At first, before we were old enough to understand the instructions or to be afraid of what we would find, before we had started to read about them, we just laid them out and looked at them or picked one secret card from the whole overturned deck and tried to guess what it was. We'd sit cross-legged with our foreheads together and the person with the card would think about it as hard as she could and the other would guess. We sat like that for hours sometimes. And sometimes it worked.

"The Queen of Cups," Claudia said. "That's you." The queen is blond, crowned. She sits on a throne with cupids on it and she's holding a gold cup. But I never felt like the Queen of Cups. She seemed so womanly, so beautiful and peaceful.

Later, we found out she is "beautiful, fair, dreamy—as one who sees visions in a cup . . . also wisdom, virtue."

When I was thirteen, the first cups broke. I was sitting in the kitchen alcove with my knees up and my head between my knees. There was something wet between my legs and this stirring inside of me—blood for the first time. I was rocking back and forth, nauseous, but I wasn't making any sounds. I remember it was a hot day. My mother was marketing. My father had gone to work in his study.

There was a crashing sound, then another. I felt it deep in my molars and shivering along the edge of my front teeth—the smash of china into fragments. When it was finally quiet, I went into the dining room. In the dining room are the mahogany cabinets that my mother's parents brought with them when they came from Europe. The Nazis wouldn't let them take money so they brought the cabinets instead. My mother loves them and fills them with her best china— "bone china." As a child I wondered what that meant. Like bone. Made of bone. Anyway, that day I was thirteen, some cups had fallen out of the cabinets and smashed in white and pink and blue bits on the floor.

I ran across the street to Claudia's house and sat on her bed and cried. I told her about the broken china cups, how I thought I had broken them.

"See," Claudia said, "you are the Queen of Cups."

"I don't think so," I said. "I think she puts things together, not breaks them."

My mother once told me about the haunted villa where she had stayed when she went to study painting in Italy. She used to be a painter, my mother, before she married my father, and she was beautiful. I've seen pictures. She looked like Botticelli's Venus with her long neck and hair and opally skin. While she was staying in Italy, my mother met this Italian boy at the Trevi Fountain. "He was drinking a lemon soda and he had the face of one of those half-man half-goat things—those fauns," my mother said. He took her to the countryside where he lived with his family of nine brothers and sisters and that night my mother and he made love on the dining-room table while everyone slept.

On the bus ride home, she had been dizzy and shaking in the heat. The villa was quiet. My mother went into the kitchen that faced a courtyard and made some pasta. I imagine the pasta was made with basil and garlic and the courtyard was sunny and filled with flowers and herbs. When she sat down to eat, her hands were shaking and suddenly she looked up and saw six thick white china plates leap in an arc out of the cabinet and smash on the tiled floor.

The villa was known to have been haunted for centuries by the ghost of a beautiful girl. The girl had been so beautiful that men had come from everywhere to try to marry her. Her father, crazed with jealousy, had raped her, and the girl, in revenge, had hired an assassin. After the father's death, the mother had the girl tried and she was hanged. Her bones were buried in the basement and strange things had been happening for centuries—strange shadows, whispers, broken mirrors, broken plates.

I remembered that story and looked at Claudia.

"I am afraid," I said.

Claudia put her arms around me and I buried my face in her curls. "I wish you could use that power to break him," Claudia said.

Even now, Claudia calls me the Queen of Cups.

We are walking around the lake in the evening and the lake is the color of water in a dream—too blue, too dark, too still. The air smells of pine. We are high on some pot Claudia stole from one of Eva's jars.

"Do you see visions in cups?" Claudia asks me. "Can you tell me who I will fuck next?" She laughs.

"Fill it with enough booze and I'll tell you anything," I say.

We are standing on the bridge looking down into the water. I am imagining what it would feel like to jump off the bridge, feeling the sweat cooling on my skin as I fall.

I don't want to close my eyes because I feel like I might see something. Sometimes, when I close my eyes, I see Claudia wrapped in bandages like a mummy with just her mouth showing.

"I'm not the Queen of Cups," I say. "But you're that other card—that High Priestess. 'Secrets, mystery,' and you look just like her." Claudia's little pointed face, big eyes. She would wear a horned crown like that and carry a crescent moon if she could find them in a thrift store.

Claudia says, "One of those Tarot expert guys says the High Priestess's perfume is menstrual blood. Pretty scary."

"I could use some of that," I say.

"You've just got to cool out. And eat. Look how skinny you are. They say when your body's under stress, your period's the first thing to go. We should get out of here. Go to Italy or something. The sexiest men in the world. Gods, I'm serious. And they've got that art. Botticelli and everything. We'd fatten you up on loads of pasta and wine. What are you afraid of anyway?"

I think of women with fat clotted at their bellies, thighs, buttocks. Hemorrhaging blood. But I won't tell Claudia. I think of fairies without breasts and they're floating out of the throat of the calla lily, white as calla lily flesh, wet from the throat of the flower.

"'Secrets and mystery,'" Claudia says. "Look into your cup and reveal them, then."

I don't want to see Claudia's future—or anyone's. I'm not the Queen of Cups. But I imagine someday living in a house full of light with a terraced garden spilling passion flowers into a patio—a house by the sea, full of light. I would always be able to be in water then. When we went to Jamaica, I was in water every day, every single day. My mother had to practically drag me from the water. I thought, how could I not be in water every day? It is like sleep. Better. It is better than food that can fatten or sleep that can haunt. It is like breathing. But better. I got to snorkel, to see the huge purple fish face-to-face just under the surface. My legs looked tiny and helpless and blue under the water. The fish glowed like lanterns and, at first, every time I saw one, I inhaled water and came up sputtering. But pretty soon I learned. I swam like a glowing fish.

"Look," Claudia says now and we see a deer alert at the side of the road, stopping for a moment before it disappears into the trees.

Maybe someday I'll live by water so I can heal myself every day. I will grow a garden filled with passion flowers, lilies, iris, hibiscus, also with shells.

I had a dream about making love to Jack inside a shell and his hair was dark from water —

sea-black hair—his eyelashes clumped thicker from water; his cheekbones felt like half-shells when I pressed my mouth to them.

Maybe next time I see him, I'll tell him about the dream. And about how someday I want a house with a kitchen in the center filled with children and animals bringing in sand with them, surfboards on the porch, pots of rice on the stove, a house with a garden and a glass room overlooking the ocean. A studio with shell cups to mix my paints in. Those kind of cups I'll look into.

Maybe I'll tell him.

THE STAR.

"This is beneath him. It is his own—that which he has to work with and can use."

IV. The Star

My mother has two silk roses in her cabinet. Nijinsky wore them when he danced in *The Specter of the Rose*. My mother used to take one out and let me hold it. It looked and felt like a real rose but it smelled like old closets, old silk. We have a photograph of Nijinsky as the Specter. His eyes are closed and his eyelids and lips look like petals. Sometimes, I would find my mother holding the rose or the photograph and crying.

We decide to have a *Midsummer Night's Dream* full-moon party. My mother brings out all her white tulle and we hang it in the trees. We cut out paper stars and glue blue and pink glitter onto them and scatter them in the tulle canopies among white Christmas lights. We buy watermelons, pineapples, cantaloupes, honeydew, strawberries and cut them up and put them on platters and my mother makes her punch. It is a citrus-greenish-yellow color and it smokes. We call it the witch brew and everyone is drinking and dancing around in their white shirts and dresses and lace and masks and glittery scarves. I am smoking and carrying calla lilies. Claudia hates those flowers because, she says, they remind her of wax-faced corpses, funerals and death.

I am hoping that Jack will come and I keep looking for him. I am biting my lip remembering the way he caught my lip like fruit. Everyone looks very pale, washed white in the moon and drained white from the punch. It is cold but it makes you sweat, that witches' brew. Everyone is white with a greenish cast like my lilies.

Claudia's mother, Eva, is standing on a chair waving her arms over her head. She is wearing a full caftan and her arms look like wings. She is quoting Shakespeare: "'So quick bright things come to confusion.'" Some people are tangled up by the fountain at the base of the garden. You can hear the murmurs and sometimes you can see a bare limb, pale and disembodied, coming out of the bushes. Claudia has taken off her top and is joining them.

I am waiting behind my lilies wishing Claudia would cover her chest and come back. I stare into the porch light and then look away, seeing an image of Claudia on the dark air, a Claudia ghost wrapped in bandages, just her mouth showing. Jack, I think, wanting him to kiss the picture out of my eyes.

Then I see him looking out into the garden from the house. His face framed in the window. He is wearing a wreath of leaves and roses and he looks like an elf. Because of his slanted eyes, the panther tilt of his cheekbones and because he is laughing. I haven't seen him laugh before.

I go into the house but I can't find him. I look in all the rooms. There are the wooden Jamaican men. There is Zack in his covered cage. The green velvet chair. The lamps covered with pink scarves. People waiting in line for the bathroom. The bowls of steaming green brew. The tall flowers—gladiolas, lilies—the bowls of wet fruit. The people twisted together on the bed. The people dancing. Jungle Jim's bald head. Cherie's bleached white tease. Charlie in sunglasses. Victoria unbuttoning her blouse.

Perdita is wearing antique lace, and feathers in her hair. She is wearing strands of beads, a plastic necklace filled with green glow-in-the-dark liquid and a glass bird ring. She is dancing by herself and when she sees me, she comes and takes my hand.

We dance together, swinging our hands and

our skirts like wings. Perdita looks like she is floating because her dress is so long and white and her legs are so delicate and seem almost boneless the way she drifts back and forth to the music. She holds up her arms and I swing her around.

I feel like when I was little before I was afraid all the time. Dancing and swirling the silk of my skirt. Perdita has stars pasted on her face. They catch the light. I am six and a half with her, loving my body because it can dance, because it is my body, for a moment not even knowing what it is like not to love my body. I am also her mother. I am aware of a weightiness beneath my belly but I don't hate it. I imagine that Perdita is my child, that I dress her in lace and scarves and flower wreaths and we go out and dance in the park, play Goddess and Egypt, that I show her paintings and we draw with colored chalk on the sidewalk, that I read her fairy tales and feed her fruit and bread and milk.

I imagine that Perdita is my child and that together we can be children and that, dancing, we are butterflies spreading our silk butterfly skirts, unfolded from cocoons, but still protected, safe.

I kiss Perdita and go back outside. She is still dancing.

"You are a star, Laurel," I hear him say. "You are a star," and he takes my chin in his hand and licks my lips, tastes them the way you lick salt off the rim of a margarita glass.

We go back inside — up the spiral stairs to my tower room. He starts rubbing himself with his hand. He is still wearing the wreath. I think I recognize the roses.

"I want you to take off your dress," he says.

I crouch on the bed. I let my petticoat dress slip off my shoulders. Then I pull it up, starting at the center of the hem, which is draped between my knees. He comes over and takes my dress and twists it into a cord. Then he ties my wrists together above my head. His head is between my legs—a garden of leaves and roses between my thighs. I recognize his lips, even far away in the darkness.

I keep sighing, trying to get the words out. "I never come," I say finally.

"It's okay. Just relax." He puts his palms on my stomach.

We lie still in my bed under the ceiling painted with stars.

"What were you dreaming?" he asks. He is holding my wrists. "You were waving your arms in front of your face and crying."

"I'm afraid," I say. "I think about that man that's been climbing in windows at night and raping women and cutting their throats. I can't even listen to the news anymore."

He holds me close. He says, "Why are you so obsessed with death?"

I say, "I dressed up like Death's bride for

Halloween once. I bought a wedding dress with all this train at a thrift store. It was stained and I dyed it black. I painted my face white."

"Death's bride," he says, stroking my hair.

"I saw this man at Cannon's the other night. He was gorgeous—he must have been a model. But under his tan and everything you could see he was dying. He was walking with a cane and smoking like crazy and shaking. He was young and gorgeous and dying from something in his blood. I can't even listen to the news hardly.

"I saw my father eaten by disease. At first it was like a fire and then he started to look like ashes. His eyes and his skin started to look like ashes. . . . "

"You should paint," Jack says.

"I used to draw and paint all the time." I painted beasts and fairies and elves, china dolls with worlds in their eyes and chests. I lay on the cool floor for hours, biting my lip, twirling my hair around my finger with my free hand, drawing.

"You should paint everything. What you feel. All your demons." His voice sounds tender; his voice sounds full, too full for his throat, and tender.

"I should paint you then," I say. "Demons."

He looks up from under the arch of his brows. "You should paint all of us," he says.

"I always wanted to paint a deck of Tarot cards with everyone's face in it," I say. "My mother would be the Moon. Claudia would be the High Priestess. Perdita would be the Star. And the Magician . . . my father would be the Magician."

"What would I be?" Jack asks.

"The Devil. The Devil with hooves who keeps lovers in chains. Also the Lover."

"And you? Who are you?"

I think for a moment. "The Hanged Man," I say.

"This is behind him. It is the current from which he is passing away, and it may be the past of the matter."

V. IX of Swords

At this party downtown, the loft floors are spattered with fluorescent paints that glow in the black lights. People are wearing black so they disappear in the black lights or fluorescent orange and green so they glow like the floor or white so they startle like teeth. Some black men from the bar down the street have wandered in to watch and ask some bleach blondes to dance but no one will dance with them so they stand around drinking and snickering, leaning against the walls. Everyone else is part of the usual crowd, pale and smoking.

I look for Jack, feeling an emptiness inside me. I crush my cigarette with my pump heel and light another. Do I look okay? I stroke my hips—jutting bones beneath my dress. I touch my hair, my throat. I want him to tell me I am beautiful.

"I dreamed about you the other night," he says, coming over. "I'm glad you're here. Are you all right?"

"Yes. Why?"

"I dreamed you were in this buzzing blue neon room sitting up in bed and crying and there were swords above you in the air. I wanted to call and see how you were."

"The Nine of Swords," I say, blowing smoke.

"We need to get away from here," Jack says. "Drive to Mexico, shave our heads and drink mescal. Or go to Guatemala and live in a tent with some parrots and snakes and dress in colors like the Indians. We need to get some sun on this white flesh. We need to get into some water. You need to be in water," he says, stroking my forehead. "Let's get out of here." And he takes my hand.

He puts his helmet on me and squeezes my thighs. "Are you on?"

The motorcycle is huge. I cling to him the whole way with the night charging against us.

I smell the ocean before I see it shining and black in the distance. We park the bike and go down to the sand, not saying anything, just breathing. There are a few stars.

"Well you can tell what it's telling you," he says, finally. "About giving and taking and letting go." Watching the waves. "Let's go in," he says.

"No way."

"Come on." He starts to undress. "Just a little. I'll hold you. Come on."

He runs naked to the edge of the water and dives into a wave. It breaks and the water licks out onto the sand, a spit of foam whitening in the starlight. I look for him, my heart beating. Then he rises up, gleaming. "Come on! Come here!"

I go nearer, laughing, standing at the edge of the water. "It's so cold. I'm scared. No way. Jack . . . "

But he is already coming toward me. I taste salt water as it drips off his hair. It's like the night has turned to liquid and is beading off him onto my face and lips. The black wet salt crystal night. I scream as he lifts me up and carries me into the water. A wave rises above us. I remember when I was little, how my father held me like this while I kicked and screamed and the wave broke over us. Choked with water. But now the wave carries us out gently, lifting our bodies and in Jack's arms I am light. I am foam. Mermaid.

As the water quiets, he kisses me. The closest I have come to coming since I was fourteen.

My father had taken me down to the bottom of the garden. We sat among the spiny purple flowers at the bottom of the garden and my father was telling me a story. He told me about the beast who loved the beautiful girl. "The Beast was very wise and good but he was a beast. He had hairy hands and a hairy head full of teeth. But he loved Beauty. And, finally, when she loved him back, he turned into a prince."

It was hot, even at the bottom of the garden. It smelled of summer and the air had that crackle. The fountain was broken and the water lay still and mossy green in the basin. If we had kept fish there, they would have been dead, floating belly up, glowing a faint orange in the water. Maybe there were fish, dead in the basin. But I don't remember for sure.

I remember about Beauty and the Beast and the hall of hands and the magic mirror and the rose that Beauty's father picked. When Beauty's father picked that rose, Beauty belonged to the Beast. Forever.

My father took me to a carnival once. He bought me pink spun-sugar candy and I wanted a dress like that. We rode the Ferris wheel and my father pointed out the city to me—the hills and the palm trees and pastel houses. We spun in teacups until we felt sick. Then we went into the fun house. In the fun house I saw myself fat, horribly fat, squat and fat. And I fell in the rolling barrel in the fun house and I couldn't get up for what seemed like a long time. I rolled around and around shrieking in the barrel. My father stood on the other side, watching me. Then he put out his big, delicate hand and helped me up.

He said, "Oh, you weren't really afraid?"

There was a fat, chewing man sitting in front of a haunted house. There was a wizard in a starry hat painted on the outside of the haunted house. My father took my hand. He said, "You'll like this one."

I had to walk into the dark, into a dark darker than any I had ever been in. So dark that it was like the dark I imagine inside my body, as if there were no difference between the dark inside of me and the dark outside, as if I had stopped existing. It was a dark that twisted and turned, clanked and rattled and smashed around us. Twice it broke enough to show us a bald mannequin missing an eye and some horrible, tubular, gas-masked thing behind bars. I felt hands touching me in the impossible dark.

That is what wakes me sometimes, even now, wakes me in the middle of the night so I sit straight up, with my face in my hands. That is what wakes me so I sit straight up like the woman in the card called the Nine of Swords. There are nine swords pointed horizontally above and behind her. This is the card of "death, failure, miscarriage, delay, deception, disappointment, despair."

Sometimes I wonder what it would have been like to have had the child.

Eddie Flynn was so beautiful—like a girl almost with his curls and huge green eyes, the longest eyelashes. People teased him because he was so pretty. We met in art class while we were putting our hands in the wet clay making animals. Eddie was making a lion with wings and a human head—a sphinx. We talked the whole time; Eddie didn't talk much to anyone else. And everyone else talked about parties and their tans and getting suspended and sometimes about drugs. I remember thinking—when the fat greasy-haired girl said, "angel dust"—I remember thinking it sounded so beautiful. Angel Dust. Before I heard about kids drowning in their bathtubs and trying to cut out their eyes from smoking it.

Eddie and I talked about painting and camping and books. Eddie's favorite books were *The Little Prince* and anything science fiction. He showed me his drawings—these intricate sci-fi fantasies with flying saucers and creatures, sorcerers and women with constellations in their eyes and rivers in their hair. He worked on a tiny scale covering huge surfaces and labeling everything with mysterious phrases and symbols printed tiny, tiny at the bottom of the page. I think he really believed in the whole thing. He said he'd been having dreams about exploding stars since he could remember—"the colors, and stars like powdered sugar donuts and my head was a bubble of glass."

Eddie told me how his mother was crazy and

always had different men over and screamed and ate candy between the men. And how once she tried to kill herself and he had to clean up all the blood from her wrists off the bathroom floor. I didn't tell him about my family, but I think he knew. He met my father once. I invited him over after school and we were eating ice cream in the kitchen. And my father came in from his study and stood there looking at us. He didn't say anything, just looked at us—first at Eddie and then at me and then he went to the sink and began to wash his hands very, very carefully as if he were washing off something that disgusted him. And then he looked at us again with his eyes narrowed and he walked out of the room.

Eddie used to say how all he wanted was to get out of this place, out of this school and away from these people, maybe go to Europe and see the art, go to Italy and see the marble sculptures. He said he thought he would get really sick if he stayed here. He said I should come with him.

We left school early and walked up the fire road into the Hollywood hills. Sometimes we saw someone on a horse but mostly it was empty up there. It smelled of pine and you could hear coyotes sometimes, see deer. Eddie walked with his head down, his curls falling into his eyes, his hands in his pockets and he kicked up the dust with his sneakers. He spoke very softly and because his head was down, his shoulders hunched, he looked even smaller than he was.

"I think the world is so fucked up," Eddie said. His voice was always soft and crackly as if he were about to cry.

We were sitting under the eucalyptus tree looking out over the smoggy blue hills and the lake reflecting the clouds. It smelled of earth and pot; Eddie had lit a joint. Eddie had showed me about getting high and it was so sweet, like all the pain just turned to sweet smoke and blew right out of me, leaving me hungry for chocolate ice cream. Everything was chocolate ice cream and kisses and wind. I remember that he was so gentle and warm, it was like holding an animal—all that perfect radiance filling up the animal and moving right into you, right into you through the chill of your skin. That was what it was like holding him under the eucalyptus tree.

So maybe it was Eddie's baby; maybe it would have been Eddie's baby that I would have had. Even though we didn't do all that much. But they say it can happen.

I had only had a few periods then. So when I was late I didn't think much about it. But finally I had to tell my mother. I felt strange—my breasts so full and I threw up a couple of times and there was a heavy, mysterious feeling just beneath my belly. And when I told my mother she screamed, "Why didn't you tell me? Why didn't you tell me what you've been doing? We would have gotten you birth control. Oh God."

"But just don't tell Dad. Please don't tell him."

He found out though and I remember his face. It looked ashy the way it looked later on when they found out he had the disease. And his eyes looked very hot, volcanic, and he didn't say too much. He just said, "It's that kid. That one that looks like a fag. You won't be seeing him anymore."

I felt dizzy for a few days—tender, bloodless. I told Eddie but I thought it would be okay. I thought he would say, "The world is so fucked up." I thought we would sneak off into the hills and sit in the branches of the eucalyptus and get high and talk. He was the only person, besides Claudia, I wasn't afraid to have touch me.

But Eddie got quiet when I told him. "I don't think it could have been me," he said. "I don't know who it was. . . . " He walked away from me after art class. The semester was almost over and he hardly ever spoke to me after that.

I saw him once, standing on a street corner wearing tight white jeans and smoking a cigarette. I heard later that he'd dropped out of school, that some old guy had taken him to Europe. I think about him sometimes, about the way he walked, looking down and kicking up dust.

Sometimes I think about what it would have been like to have had a baby then. I still feel like one now. It would have been a babies' baby all pale and bruised and breakable-looking. It would have terrified me, that baby. I can't even imagine it pressing out of me. I think of horror stories on the news, like that girl who waited and waited, keeping the pregnancy secret and then threw the newborn baby out of a window eight flights up. I imagine how much she must have hated herself to do that. I imagine having a little girl that looks like Perdita, dancing with a little girl; I wish you could give your kids invisible armor when they're born. I think about the beautiful boys on the streets in their tight jeans. I think about Eddie Flynn kicking up the dust and about his distant, dreamy eyes.

I wonder if his body hurts him sometimes in the night the way mine used to hurt me. I see him lying on the edge of a bed wincing and holding himself. Going into the hills above Florence and looking out over the green misty city with Michelangelo's David all perfect beside him. All perfect and complete and untouched.

"This is before him. It is the current that is coming into action and will operate in the specific matter."

VI. VII of Cups

The ground and the walls of the buildings in St. Elmo's Village are painted in red, yellow, and green — the colors of Africa. There are flowers and faces, Rastafarians with dreadlocks, turbaned women, fish and birds and waves painted on the ground and on the walls. Within this painted world, the street fair sings and dances and beats its drums. Men in African shirts and sunglasses are playing music — it would be orange if it were a color. Two women in turbans are dancing. Claudia and I stand in front of the stage, swaying our hips. Claudia is wearing a sarong skirt and a big black hat and African beads and she is eating a piece of sweet potato pie that makes her voice sound thick and sweet. Children are roller-skating around.

After the men leave the stage, tiny girls with beaded braids do a dance to "Egyptian Lover." They turn their heads profile and flatten their palms to the sky like Egyptian wall paintings. I wish I were one of them.

I know that Perdita wishes she were too. She runs up to us and throws her arms around my legs. I lift her up; she has a tiny paper parasol in her hair and lipstick smeared on her mouth but it looks like smudges of watermelon candy. A beautiful Rastafarian man with the eyes and nose of a wild cat walks by and looks at us. Perdita is watching the dancing girls, mesmerized.

"You are going to be a dancer, aren't you?" I say to Perdita. I look into her eyes and see stars like the stars she wears pasted on her cheeks sometimes. I see her on a stage and dressed in white, dressed in white and wings.

Perdita nods, rubbing her mouth with the back of her hand, never taking her eyes off the dancing girls.

When they are done, I put her down.

She lets go of my hand and runs up to the stage where the next band is setting up. A man bends down and lifts her in his arms. She is giggling and pulling on his jacket collar. In the strong sunlight I see their faces. The same shell cheekbones, small noses, the same too-pale skin. Why hadn't I noticed before how much they look alike. It is Jack and Perdita. I leave Claudia and go to him.

"A pleasure as always," he says, kissing my hand. "What do you think of it here?"

"It's great," I say. "I feel good. Are you playing?"

"Drums with these guys," Jack says, gesturing. "They teach me a lot. Make it pulse. Make them feel their pulse. Like they've been running. Or making love. Use what you see for that. It will save you. Maybe art will save you." Then he laughs. "Right, Dita?" Messing up her hair.

"Maybe it would have saved my parents," I say. "But they just stopped. My father made these really cool sculptures and my mother was a painter. Really good. But they both stopped."

When my mother was studying art in Italy, she used to work with tiny, precise brush strokes and she was always so quiet, so shy, with her cramped fingers, terrified of things. The professor was a huge man, eight feet tall, my mother said, he seemed eight feet tall and old, an Italian with hands like sides of meat or slabs of marble, my mother said. One day, he came over to her and took the brush, pried it from her fingers and painted wildly in red over what she had made and kept painting then, did not stop but kept painting all over the walls of the studio and on the door, down the hall, the class following him, speechless, and my mother's tears drying from the shock of it. And he didn't stop until he reached the outside walls, by this time red and wild-eyed and sweating. "A madman," my mother said. "Oh God, I hated him, I loved him," my mother said.

But she stopped painting. Ever since my father. I still wonder what it was she had made that day, so tiny in the center of the canvas and what she painted after that Italian swept her along like paint herself. I have only seen the picture in the hall of the kneeling woman. I think she is the woman from the haunted villa where my mother stayed in Italy when the cups broke. The woman whose father raped her. The eyes follow you with tiny light windows, broken mirrors. I wonder if it would have been different if my mother had kept painting. Instead she cleans and cooks and laughs, calls herself a Gypsy witch. And if my father had kept making the bronze women. If that would have changed him.

"Don't you stop," Jack says. "Use what you see so you don't start hurting yourself with it."

I think of the card called the Seven of Cups. A man is in silhouette, his back turned, one hand out and he's looking at a cloud with seven gold cups on it. Out of each rises an image—a head, a draped figure, a snake, a castle, jewels, a laurel wreath, a fork-tongued creature. "Strange chalices of vision. Fairy favours . . . imagination." I wonder if these are what the Queen of Cups would see if she looked into her cups.

Sometimes I think that the same thing in me that smashed all that glass and china is what can see things. Sometimes if I look into someone's eyes, it is like looking into water reflecting what will be, what they will become.

In Perdita's eyes I see stars—tiny stars of loss, abandonment, also hope and promise. I see Perdita on a stage, wearing white.

In Claudia's eyes I have seen the High Priestess's horned crown. I have seen Claudia wrapped in gauze. Claudia's arms are bruised.

My mother's eyes are strange moons.

Once, as my father stood over me, I saw blades reflected in his eyes.

Sometimes I have seen what will be, what someone will become. Maybe that is why Jack keeps his sunglasses on. I see only myself reflected in the lenses, myself alone and in a mirror darkness.

I am a mirror. I have seen myself alone in my

reflected eyes. But I am surrounded by gold cups out of which rise jewels, wreaths, demons.

"I've got to set up now, baby," Jack says to Perdita, putting her down. "I'll see you later. And you too. We'll go out to eat or something. You look skinny. I think you could use some dinner." He is looking at me, I think. He has his sunglasses on.

I take Perdita's hand and we go back to Claudia.

After a while, the band starts to play. Jack is beating on the drums with his hands but also with everything. It's in his chin and neck and shoulders, back, thighs, calves and in the blood pumping through everything. And I feel the drums like that in me too.

"Let's dance," says Claudia, taking Perdita's other hand. We all move together to the music in the red, yellow, and green heat that smells of vanilla-banana incense. I wish that I could dance with paint—cover everything, every wall, the pavement, with images, color, like this place is covered. Tilt over gold cups so the colors of our lives spill onto the pavement. In the pictures that we want to see.

THE HANGED MAN.

"Himself."

VII. The Hanged Man

My mother is cooking and cooking. She is scrubbing beets and peeling the beets and scrubbing them again. She is chopping them up with her huge knife and staining the cutting board and her hands. Then she boils the beets in a pot. She peels the flesh off the chicken and rinses the naked breasts and legs and wings (wings like someone's vulnerable back) and bakes them with pearly onions and lemons and herbs. She bakes cakes that overflow their pans, nightmarish chocolate cakes, wicked with nuts and sugar and the chocolate that people say has the same chemicals that your body releases when you are in love. She bakes these wicked love-cakes and the chocolate heats and drips and the smell fills up the house. My mother keeps salt-rubbed, sun-cured crystals in the kitchen to make sure all her ingredients are pure. "Untainted," my mother says. She takes forever doing the dishes. Rinse. Soak in boiling water. Scrub. Rinse. Rinse. She follows me around with broom and mop. My mother afraid of the disease that killed my father.

Once, I saw dark X-ray shadows around his hips and abdomen. Then they were gone.

When my mother told me that he was sick, I thought I had done it, that I had made him sick. "Cancer," my mother said.

That is different than smashing things — broken cups and saucers. Cancer. But maybe I'd done it.

Maybe I killed him, I thought. Maybe I dreamed it there in his cells.

My mother thinks it was impurities. She scrubs the vegetables; she keeps crystals in the kitchen. She chants sometimes.

I sit at the kitchen table looking at pictures of missing children. Eyes, hair, D.O.B. I drink coffee that buzzes through my blood, better than the sluggish chocolate love and I smoke. I smoke and smoke. My lipstick stains the ends of my cigarettes as if they have made my mouth bleed. The ashtrays fill with lipstick-stained butts and ashes.

Claudia says, "You smoke when you really feel like crying." I smoke and smoke. Have you ever had the sensation of losing flesh? You begin to feel the bones of your skeleton under your flesh. Bones of the shoulders. Bones of the rib cage. Bones of the hips. It is like finding a new being, one free of desire, free of time, almost.

At night, I lie awake thinking about the man who climbs in through windows and kills women. My eyes choke on the darkness and my stomach is like a live thing—a separate creature that I have imprisoned, that is under my power. It is a little painted demon howling inside me. I imagine that the reason I don't bleed anymore each month is because this demon, this lie-baby, is sucking up all the blood to feed itself, to keep itself alive. I hear horror stories about girls who don't eat—how their hair turns white and their gums bleed. But I feel beautiful, perfect. I am all pale bone and bone-pale flesh and pale hair and I am light. I am like some fairy thing. I dream about fairies dancing around the house with their rib cages showing like baskets under their flesh.

I could drift up and away from here. I am so light. Bound by nothing. Not even time. And I am pure now.

"Come with me. To eat," Jack says.

I can't believe it's him calling me—the liquor crack of his voice. It's him.

"I'll pick you up."

I go outside and light a cigarette while I wait for him. It is a quiet night and hot still.

I hear the motorcycle rounding the curve of the road and I see him pull up on it with his legs looking charged in the dark jeans. His boot heels dig into the dirt. I put out my cigarette, take the helmet he hands me, and climb on behind him.

"Hold on," he says and my hands hold just above his hips where I've gripped when he's entered me.

"Your hands are cold," he says, feeling them as his shirt slips up.

"That's so that the heat stays here. . . . " I reach around and touch his abdomen. He turns his head slightly, his mouth near mine as we ride.

We drive up behind a truck and something is hanging out of the back—shredded paper limp from the blood that has soaked it. "Carter's Meat Packing" written on the side of the truck. The night feels like something soft we are ripping open, tearing apart. It smells of meat and my perfume and the flowers. People are out on the street wearing very little. A lot of them are touching each other.

Jack says, "Mexican food?" and we skid into Lucy's parking lot.

While we wait in line in the cool candlelight, Jack touches my shoulder, my waist, my lower back—purposely, lightly, as if he is trying to figure something out. When we sit he orders margaritas and tostadas. He says, "You should eat this," and he starts to put the tostada filling into the tortilla in his hand, piling on the lettuce and cheese and guacamole. I watch him and drink some of my margarita. Icy and salty and sharp-sweet and making me feel that way you feel just as you're about to fall asleep, your body so heavy and your mind beginning to flash dream-fragments like coming attractions.

I realize how hungry I am, how my stomach feels like an empty hand making a fist to feel full but there's nothing in the fist but fingers. Jack licks his lips and touches my face with the back of his hand.

"You should eat," he says.

I take a slow bite looking down. The guacamole kisses my mouth. My throat feels tight but I swallow. Then I drink some more of the margarita.

Jack puts his hand on my thigh. "You don't have to worry," he says.

When we have finished eating we get back on the motorcycle and drive. Dizzy. Jack stops at the Safeway and tells me to wait. I sit on the motorcycle trying to look mean in the helmet so the men in cars will leave me alone. Then he comes out with a paper bag and we drive to my house. We start up the stairs, avoiding the kitchen where I hear my mother banging pots around. It smells like meat and onions.

Up in my room I light the thick green candle with the Virgin Mary and the roses on the glass. I open my windows so the room fills with summer and mint. Jack undresses me slowly, unbuttoning my blouse and jeans, pulling the leg band of my lace underwear over his head and straining till the underwear tears. He opens the paper bag and takes out a container of strawberry ice cream, a plastic spoon and a bottle of champagne. "Happy Birthday," he says. He sits behind me, placing the chilly bottle between my thighs and popping the cork off in front of us. Some champagne spills over the top onto my thighs. Jack licks it off. He hands me the bottle and I take a sip. Then he opens the ice cream container and spoons some into his mouth. When he kisses me, the strawberry ice cream slips into my throat. I try to breathe through my nose. Jack kisses ice cream onto my throat and nipples so that I shiver. He licks ice cream onto my hipbones and between my legs. He splashes champagne over me. It froths and tickles. I take some champagne from his mouth. My head feels like little champagne corks are popping inside of it.

Later in the night I wake up alone; my skin feels sticky and there is a burning between my legs. My stomach sways with nausea. I get out of bed and go into the bathroom. I put my fingers down my throat, gag, and vomit into the toilet.

Claudia and I are riding the tree like witches on brooms. We're in the big eucalyptus over the lake where Eddie and I used to go. It's like being above everything when you sit in the branches.

An electric breeze makes Claudia's hair fly out. She throws back her head, laughing.

"This tree's dangerous. The widow-maker," Claudia says. "Eva calls it that."

Claudia just read my cards. "The Hanged Man," she said. "Renunciation. Self-deprivation. Suspended in illusion. In the Egyptian deck, he is condemned to hang in hell eating his own waste. Self-poisoning. Also, resurrection."

Claudia's hands, heavy with silver, lie twitching in her lap. Her eyes look blind, blind as Eva's one blind eye.

"Self-poisoning. The poison we make and feed ourselves," she says now, gazing at the city drowning in soot and smog.

After, I go home and dream of the Hanged Man—a huge Tarot card looming out of the darkness—no, not the card, the man himself, painfully suspended, eyes rolled in his head, the slack, red mouth. Hanging in hell eating his own shit.

I wake with my fingers at my neck.

THE DEVIL.

"House, environment . . . the influence, people and events."

VIII. The Devil

Claudia and I are sitting on the lilac satin comforter that Claudia calls a coffin blanket. The light outside is the same color as the bedspread — twilight. We are listening to The Doors.

I am smoking and my lipstick-tipped cigarette butts are filling up the ashtray. Claudia's room is filled with round mirrors, dried roses, lace, and photos of old movie stars who died in strange ways. It smells of smoke and opium incense — smells that have seeped into the lace and satin, leather jackets and lingerie during the hot afternoons. The lamplight is pink because of the ballerina tutu Claudia has placed over the lampshade. I feel weak and heavy in the heat, like the hibiscus flowers hanging their heads outside Claudia's window. Claudia's room is on the ground floor and it makes me afraid for her because of the man that is breaking all those windows and raping women and cutting their throats. But Claudia keeps the windows open, even at night, so she can smell the flowers and the exhaust and hear the flock of parrots that live in the trees. These birds have escaped from their cages and they live wild now in the trees around here. Tonight we hear them screeching.

Claudia is playing with a piece of lace, holding it up with one hand, batting at it with the other like a cat.

"I met the best guy," she says. "He's a sculptor down at the beach. I was walking on the boardwalk and he saw me and goes, 'You are

Isis,' and I said, 'What?' and he said, 'You're my next piece. Isis. You know, Egypt.' He does these body casts—kind of like mummies. All white and really strange but beautiful too. And he's using me."

"Are you sleeping with him?"

"He's so sexy," Claudia says, licking her lips. "And he's going to be a famous artist. So my tits'll be famous too." She strokes her breasts and I see the nipples under her T-shirt. "He gets me some killer drugs."

"Claudia, why don't we do something. We could go to Italy and see the art. Botticelli and everything. Or do something here. Work with hurt kids. Teach them painting. We could get involved with some peace project. Or just take some art classes or something. This scene is fucking us up. We'll be witches like our mothers."

I grab her wrist and look at her arms. They

are covered with bruises like the prints of purple petals. I want to bury my face in her electric curls.

"Heroin my heroine. My boyfriend gets it for me." She gets up and goes into the bathroom, still holding the piece of lace.

The TV screen is buzzing with colored dots like an electric Impressionist painting. Like a screen full of Claudia's sparkling rhinestone earrings.

"Claudia. What the fuck are you doing?"

I follow her. She is standing over the sink tying the piece of lace around her upper arm and patting her veins to get the blood.

"Claudia, don't." I grit my teeth.

"I'm good with needles."

She slips it in. The fine tip slips right into the vein. She smiles. "My mind is an iris," she says. "My mind is the inside of an iris all purple and veiny. My mind is a room with see-through purple walls. My mind is the iris of an eye." Her eyeballs roll back in her head. "When guys use this shit they just lie there. But it makes me want to fuck."

"Claudia," I say. "I need you. I get so scared sometimes. I wish you could climb in my mind with me."

"I'll try," she says. "Tell me what you dream about."

She stretches and strokes her rib cage as if she is made of velvet and bone.

The club is dark and red. It smells like a men's room. We sit in a red vinyl booth and smoke, Claudia and I. We are wearing rhinestones and torn leather. My hair is white, whiter in the clubs; Claudia is dark and her hair is curly red-dark, smelling of roses. "Rose White and Rose Red," I say. "Remember that fairy tale?"

"Rose Red," Claudia says, smacking the lipstick on her lips. "Who gets the Prince?"

"He was a bear," I say. "I don't remember.

Maybe no one. Maybe they got each other."

Claudia touches the inside of my arm. "What do you dream?"

Jack comes onstage wearing black and big boots. His hair is slicked back. His eyes are hidden behind glass. There are some girls who play the music. Hungry girls with wild hair. And they are all around him.

I wonder if he sees me. He is facing us. If he took off his sunglasses his eyes would be right on me. I think so.

"If there's a goat-devil in hell he'd have a band like this," Claudia says.

The voice is from deep in the underground of him, smoking still. The girls with blank china faces hold their instruments like guns or blades.

Some guys are slamming around in the pit in front of the stage. Bald kids with tattoos clawing their arms and necks.

"Come on," Claudia says. "We can slam like we used to."

She pulls me up and into the crowd of slamming boys. She holds on to me waltz-style and we shove around, all elbows and knees. My hair falls into my face, wet with sweat. I can hardly see — only dizzy flashes of light and color. Claudia's dark red hair. The music is getting faster and faster and the alcohol is coursing through my blood faster and faster as I thrash around. I feel an elbow pressing into me, just below my ribs. I double over. Falling. Claudia tries to help me up but the heel of my boot catches on the hem of my dress. It is an old silk dress and the silk, thinned, weakened from my sweat, tears at the waist, tears easily, right in half. As I stand, my dress is in two. I try to hold it together. Some bald boy grabs at me. Claudia pushes him away, takes off her jacket and we tie it around my waist. She leads me to the rest room and wipes the sweat off my face. She takes the antique rhinestone pins off her collar and pins the two halves of my dress together.

"Do you want to go?" Claudia asks.

"No. I want to see him. I have to."

We go back out.

"I have a fantasy about all of us," I say.

"What?"

"The three of us," I say. "Do you think he's beautiful?"

"Yeah, sure, Laurel," Claudia says gently. But she's looking at me in a strange way. "Sure he is."

After they have left the stage, Jack comes over to our booth. "Here he comes," I tell Claudia.

"Laurel," he says. "How are you?"

"Can I have a light?" Claudia asks.

She leans across the table with her cigarette and they kiss fire and ash.

"This is Claudia," I say.

"Claudia." He puts out his hand. He holds her hand for that extra second.

"You sounded good," Claudia says. Her voice

is husky. "Would you like to come over for a drink?"

"Sure," he says. He takes a drag on his cigarette and I feel the smoke penetrating me. I will wake up smelling of smoke.

We drive Claudia's bomb-car and Jack follows on his motorcycle. His black-gloved hands grip; his thighs look like animals ready to spring.

The club is downtown and we drive through dark side streets—the warehouses, chain link, men asleep on the sidewalk, garbage in the gutters, dismantled cars. On a corner, under the sizzling electric wires, two tall black women are standing. One is wearing a bright yellow plastic miniskirt that looks like it is made from a raincoat; one is in glittery red. They are beautiful, moving in slow motion, it seems, dreamily, leaning against each other, shoulder to shoulder, then apart. One throws back her head, her eyes closed. I see her neck in the street lamplight, straining. She takes something—a needle—and she shoots it into her neck. Her head falls forward, as if in slow motion, some dance, her dark hair falling forward around her face.

We get on the freeway and from here the buildings shine. As if there is beauty.

There are no lights on in Claudia's house when we reach the top of the canyon. Eva must be asleep. We go in the back way and step lightly, finding Claudia's room in the dark. We sit on her satin quilt.

"Do you know about Rose White and Rose Red?" Claudia asks Jack.

"Tell me."

"They were sisters. They met this bear."

Jack laughs. "Has Laurel been telling you stories about me?"

"Who gets the bear?" Claudia asks me. "Rose White or Rose Red?"

"They both do," I say.

"I think I like this story," says Jack. "You must be Rose Red," he says to Claudia. "I think the point was for them to blend together, for Rose White to get a little wilder and for Rose Red to cool down."

"Never," says Claudia, laughing.

"What about you, Rose White?" Jack asks.

"I'm trying," I say.

"But you still won't eat chocolate or meat or anything." Claudia pinches me, teasing.

"And you deny your violence," Jack says. Then he looks at Claudia. "And you pretend you're not delicate too."

I'm afraid that Claudia will never cool down, that she will keep shooting up junk into her sinewy arms, keep fucking whoever is transformed by the drug and the night into someone she's been dreaming of for a long time.

Claudia says, "We might as well have as many orgasms as we can while we can. I mean, everyone is going to get that disease anyway at this rate. No matter what we'll die anyway or maybe just blow up."

I see her getting older and crazier like Eva, like my mother. All the magic we believe in becoming madness. Delirium. I see the horned crown in Claudia's dark eyes. I want it to wash away with tears leaving her irises clear like the deer we saw at the lake.

Jack is standing above us and he pulls on Claudia's curls so her head falls back. I see his legs straining and his erection. He leans down and kisses Claudia's lipsticky mouth. She seems to soften under him, to kind of wilt like roses in the heat. I stand, thinking about each breath; I want the night outside the window, far away in the hills, I want to lie in the leaves.

"Rose White," Jack says, looking up.

"Rose White," Claudia murmurs, calling me.

She gets up and takes my hand, leads me to the bed.

"I'm trying. I'm with you. Tell me what you dream."

"I love you, Claudia."

She sits down, pulling me next to her. There are tears in her eyes. We sit looking at Jack.

It will be the three of us. I will be the mother, giving my breasts. I will be the lover, flexing my legs. The daughter, sucking milk flesh. I will be Rose White, breasts like the fleshy undersides of petals. Rose Red, unfolding red lipstick red blood red. I will be thorns. I will be the bear, massive and furred. I will be the mother, lover. I will be the daughter of the bear.

THE LOVERS.

"Hopes and fears."

IX. The Lovers

My mother tells me that my father said to her, "I only love a very few. First, there's my love for you and Laurel. But that's like one thing, almost."

He photographed me stroking a baby goat at the petting zoo. I remember that. White. Soft. He photographed me dancing with scarves. And on Halloween, dressed up like a Gypsy in my mother's jingly earrings and shawls. The skull from Mexico is in the background. My father had set up a haunted house for me.

My first memory is of him holding me up to

the light that poured through the window. He held me above the piano and made my toes play the keys.

My mother said, "When you were a baby, we were all so happy. I only had one dress then. Your father made sculptures of me naked when I was thin. He was going to be a famous artist. Before the teaching. He was so good. We had a bird named Orpheus and fruit trees in the yard. Amaryllis and iris and roses grew by themselves. Not just that oleander. Your father and I used to laugh. We'd say it was paradise.

"Now there's these moths everywhere," my mother says. "I think it's him, his spirit, something."

He was so tall and his hands could do anything. Big, delicate hands. He performed magic tricks with cards, silver rings, paper flowers. When he was young, he had made sculptures of bald, naked women with erect nipples. He could cure my fevers with cold baths, chilled blueberries in a glass, and stories about mermaids. And when I was cold, pressing his mouth to my gooseflesh; sometimes I thought he could have melted metal with his heat.

I loved my father. I adored him and feared him. I would sweat and crumple when I was near him like roses in the heat. I loved my father.

And I wanted to freeze naked, cold bronze like those women he made. Captive. But impenetrable.

I wake to a tap at the window—all the blood caught in my heart, all the breath caught in my throat, thinking of the man who breaks through windows at night and rapes those women and cuts them. Women in the hills. That is what I think of when I hear the tap on the window and see the silhouette of the man.

I can't move. I just sit here and then I see the slant of the cheekbones and the hunch of the shoulders and I see that it is Jack. He has climbed the tower.

He climbs in, into my arms. I feel the muscles bunching in his back; his back is wet. We are on the bed. His eyes are set deep in shadow as if there are held-back tears darkening beneath the surface of his skin.

He kisses me and I imagine being in a pink shell like the ones from Jamaica—the murmur of water flooding our ears. I whisper into the curve of his ear, "I dreamed we were making love in a shell."

"Mmmm . . . Don't listen to me if I talk in my sleep. I might tell you I love you. Sometimes I talk about babies in my sleep."

"Perdita and you look alike," I say.

"That's a compliment."

"Yes. She's beautiful. I want a kid like that sometime."

It is so hot in the bed. It feels like our bodies should be giving off some incandescence. I know I won't be able to find that secret coolness on the other side of the pillow. That coolness I used to find as a kid when I was sleepless in the heat. None of that. Our bodies have lit the whole bed.

"I'm so hot."

"You *are*!"

He breathes cool onto my breasts. He smells of the crushed mint from below my window.

"I dreamed your face was in this rosebush. The petals opened and it was your face," he says.

I feel like that—a rose, that his thumb and fingers between my legs are gently pushing back the petals.

"Have you seen Rose Red?" he asks.

"No. I'm so afraid for her."

"When you get strong you can help her."

As he comes, I feel a pressure release in me and before I can stop it I am crying. My whole body.

"What did he do to you?" Jack asks as his body relaxes. He strokes my head; my hair is pressed damp against my skull.

I remember the smell of hot roses.

I remember the bed with the huge posts. I remember the draperies on the bed like bride's veils. My parents' bed. My mother is not there.

"He touched you, didn't he?" Jack says. "Your father."

My father. After the first time, there wasn't blood anymore. It didn't hurt so much. And once there were little pulses of pleasure. That must have been the time—the spasms drawing his sperm back up into me. One of those seeds had made me. I never came anymore after that with anyone. What kind of baby would we have made? Twice born. Some monster with beautiful eyes like patinaed bronze.

I try to turn away and cover my mouth but it is welling up in me like an animal, like a beast with hooves. Jack grabs my wrist. He will not let me cover my mouth.

"Get rid of it."

I am screaming—all the plates and glasses

and mirrors I have ever broken are smashing around inside of me, flung against the insides of me. I imagine a storm of broken, glinting bits tearing at me.

I pull away and bury my face in the pillows. I am screaming a storm of blood and broken glass and china.

Finally, quieter.

I think of Jack—his eyes watching me. If he would press me to him, lick the wounds.

"Who are you?" I say and suddenly I feel like I can't breathe. Fear like fingers whitening to the bone as they close my throat.

The room is dark, very quiet. The air smells charred. He is gone.

"What will come."

X. Strength

I haven't seen Claudia since the night we were with Jack. I heard she is still hanging around with the sculptor she met at the beach. He does body casts of her in white plaster. Makes her look like a war casualty. He can get her junk and coke. One of his models shot herself in the head with her father's hunting rifle.

I haven't seen Jack. I look for him everywhere but I never see him. I go to parties and down to the clubs. I wake up sweating in the middle of the night, sit straight up in bed with his voice echoing inside of me.

In the day the sun never comes through. But it's so hot. Sweat in my eyes; sweat drips down my neck, beads on my nipples. It is trying to storm. The sky is swollen and dirty.

Today, I go down to the pier alone. The ground is littered with hot-dog wrappers, popcorn boxes, crepe paper. This morning there was a mermaid festival. Everyone dressed like mermaids. Now it is getting dark and everyone is going home. I am wearing shorts and my flesh is bumpy with cold on my bones.

The carousel is ready to close; there is one last ride. I choose a white horse with red roses carved on his saddle. I read once that they make carousel horses sexless so no one will be offended, but if he were real, this would be a stallion. He throws back his head, his nostrils flared. I feel him between my thighs. The music starts to play.

While I ride around and around on the horse,

I look for Jack. This is a place he would be, I think. This is a time he would come up behind me, thrusting his hands against my rib cage, pulling my head back with my hair so my lips part, so my throat is naked. I watch the last few people gathering their things and going home. There is a man with a beard carrying a scepter like Neptune's. A woman wearing shells over her breasts. They are drinking beers and laughing. It is getting darker, foggy, and I feel the chill from the sea.

When I get off the carousel, I pass the mechanical fortune-teller in her booth. Her eyes are green glass balls. As I walk past, her eyes roll in her head and stop, fixed on me.

In the distance the Ferris wheel is lit up green.

There is a little girl sitting on a bench. Crying. It is Perdita. I think it is Perdita. She is wearing a long, blond wig, a woman's wig so long on her that it reaches to her feet almost. She is wearing strands and strands of beads that cover her naked chest. Her legs and feet are bound in shimmery, greenish-silver cloth sewn like a tail.

For a second, I remember the smell at the bottom of the garden, my helpless legs and arms. Thick fingers of giants.

"Where is Victoria?" I ask.

Victoria is Perdita's mother. But Perdita looks more like me. Victoria is always on something and with a different man. Sometimes she gets so fucked up she doesn't know what she's doing.

"They left," Perdita says, crying.

Victoria has gotten so fucked up sometimes that she doesn't know what she's doing. But not this fucked up. Not so fucked up that she would forget her kid. I imagine Victoria dressed like a mermaid, leaning on some man, tilting a bottle of something into her mouth as they try to find their car. "I thought you had her," someone would say later. "I thought she was with you."

"Let's go home," I say and I help Perdita out of her mermaid tail, freeing her little girl legs. She is only wearing bathing suit bottoms under the tail so I give her my sweater which is long on her like a dress and I carry her because she is barefoot. We throw the tail and the wig into the trash on the pier and take the bus back.

My mother comes up to my room with a tray of strawberries and plain yogurt, a piece of fresh-baked bread spread with honey. She puts the tray with real butterflies pressed under glass onto my bed.

"How are you?" she asks.

"Okay," I say. I think, I wonder what you would say if I told you. Would you cry like a little girl or look hard and tell me I was imagining things again? Or would you laugh hysterically, mumbling about white moths? Maybe you would say it was my fault: "You are a witch. I knew you were a witch. Born to seduce him with your sex. To make him sick."

"I've been worried, Laurel," she says. "About you. I've been thinking we should find someone to talk to. And later, when you're feeling better maybe we can send you to Italy or someplace for a while. If you want. There's this program like the one I was in. Outside Rome. They teach you painting and stone carving. It might be really good."

I imagine pink granite, green marble, black-veined Carrara marble. Out of the stone, women waken, stretch, raise their arms, press their hands to their bellies. Full women with breasts, hips, sloping baby-sized abdomens. Not the women my father made — blind, rigid women caught in the cages of their bodies. I imagine sitting in a plaza at twilight eating pasta and drinking wine, the marble statues gleaming, looming in the soft light. I imagine painting a tower, a magician, a moon — red as pomegranates, blue as star-cloaks, veins of gold.

"I'm worried," she says. There are tears in her eyes.

I look at her, trying to imagine her young. Botticelli's Venus. I imagine him, my father, seeing her for the first time, modeling for his art class. Seeing her full of something he wanted. And how later when he could no longer capture her in clay and bronze, when she was consumed with her fears of impurities, he must have felt alone, so far away from her, the way I feel when the moon shines in my window at night.

"I am trying, Laurel," she says.

"You let it happen."

"I never wanted anything to hurt you."

"You let it happen."

She covers her face with her hands and rocks back and forth, back and forth. "Forgive me."

I hear Jack's voice: Let go of it, let go. And I go to her. There are no broken plates, no white moths, no animals screaming—only us.

And my mother and I hold each other, rocking back and forth together as if we are in the branches of the widow-maker tree above the lake.

❧

I have a dream and I dream that I am wandering naked in the park around Cannon's place. The flowers and the leaves are huge like fleshy, damp monsters stirring over my head. The light is strange and chlorine green. As I wander naked, I hear a sound—throaty, explosive. It is the tiger and I know I have to find the tiger. I go looking everywhere among the plants down by the water that runs along the edge of Cannon's property.

I turn, hearing something, and when I turn he is standing there, the tiger. There is blood. He has Jack's eyes. I unlock the cage and watch him limp across the water.

Awake, and the heat has broken, the sweat evaporating in the cooling air. The rain pours from a greenish sky.

On the sheet covering my body is a rose. It's still partly closed and the outside is white as a Kabuki dancer's powdered face. But the inside is fresh blood red—the red of blood before it has touched air, I think. And although they are together—this white, this red—they are completely separate too, the petals so thick that the red doesn't reflect onto the white but just seems to seep up from inside, spilling over the edge of the white petal just slightly. Rose White. Rose Red.

"I think the point was for them to blend together." I remember Jack's voice.

I feel something moist and warm between my thighs. It is not like desire. It is something else, vaguely remembered.

My fingertips are red. At first, I am frightened by the blood. Thinking of wounds, dying. Seeing it red as Claudia's red lipstick mouth, as my mother's oleander, the blood on the meat-packing paper, on a needle the junky hookers used to shoot up into their necks, as the blood of those girls that got killed by the man who came through a window. But it's none of that; it's mine. The way it's supposed to be.

I still haven't seen Claudia. I haven't seen Jack for weeks. I've been alone most of the time.

I think about Claudia's curls—how I would hide in them the way I used to bury my face in flowers when I was little. I hear her voice coated in smoke telling me to wake up. To wake from my dream. Eat something. Rose White.

I think about Jack. The rose on the bed feels cool against my skin and I remember his hands full of veins, his lips in the dark. Maybe I always thought that he would keep coming. That Claudia would stay too. That Jack would press his mouth to my throat to find the secret pool of my pulse, that he would say, "Let's get out of here," that he would break the window, break the spell, the cards scattering down around us in a torrent, whirring like wings.

I want to paint. I want to paint things that make people feel their pulse. Like drums. Like running. Like making love.

I will paint a Tarot deck — my own. I will go to the beach and find Claudia and ask her to pose for the High Priestess and the Queen of Pentacles. I will give her tea and irises and lace to tie her hair but not her arms. Some of the people in my deck will have brown skin. Some of the people will be my mother, Perdita, Eddie Flynn, Jack, my father. Some of the faces will be mine. I will be the Hanged Man, also the woman in the Lovers card, also the Queen of Cups. I will be Strength with her lion.

The Hanged Man

by
Francesca Lia Block

About This Guide

In *The Hanged Man* Francesca Lia Block, author of the acclaimed Weetzie Bat books, writes a searing novel about a taboo subject. Combining elements of magic, ancient fairy tales, and unsparing realism, Block crafts an unforgettable story of emotional death and rebirth that will invite passionate discussion. This reading guide is designed to facilitate group discussion by offering topics that focus on theme, characterization, style, and symbolism.

About This Book

Her father's death and her subsequent encounters with a mysterious man named Jack
force seventeen-year-old Laurel to confront long-
suppressed memories. Yet before this cathartic
experience can occur, Laurel must undertake a
journey of emotional self-discovery, like a character in a dark fairy tale. Tarot cards, serving
as mystical signposts that guide her progress,
preface each chapter of her story. As symbols,
these cards also offer readers an insight into
Laurel's disturbed psyche: her self-image as The
Hanged Man, a figure of renunciation and self-
deprivation, condemned to hang in hell. Laurel's
life is indeed hellish in its emotional aridity. Yet

The Hanged Man is also a figure of resurrection. Through sexual encounters with her demon lover, Jack, her concern for her self-destructive friend Claudia, and commitment to the creative power of art, Laurel gradually is able to come to terms with her feelings for her late father. In this way she finds strength and emotional rebirth. This richly complex novel examines troubling social issues through the lens of art: Block is a brilliant stylist who employs poetic imagery to create a haunting mood and somber tone. Block is also a master of setting. The lush Los Angeles canyon for which she was named is home to Laurel and serves as a metaphorical umbilical cord to the city where, with its party scene and fevered dance clubs, Laurel searches in vain for emotional redemption. *The Hanged Man* is Francesca Lia Block's most complex and challenging novel and one that invites and rewards serious discussion.

Critical Acclaim

"This intoxicating if painful work shares with Block's earlier novels a magic-tinged Los Angeles setting; emotionally charged, hip writing; and a stylized narrative construction derived from the timeless rhythms of myth and fairy tales. Disturbing but ultimately exhilarating."

— Starred Review, *Publishers Weekly*

"If Ms. Block's first novels were surprising, tasty snacks, *The Hanged Man* offers stylistic nuances for a more sophisticated palate."

— *The New York Times*

"Block's characters have a deeply affecting intensity, her settings are painted with an artist's eye, and her images are bits of poetry . . . a compelling presentation of alienation and eventual triumph."

—ALA *Booklist*

For Discussion

1. In her novel *Weetzie Bat*, Block describes love as "a dangerous angel." What does that mean in the context of this novel? What does *The Hanged Man* suggest about the equation of love and sex and of love and death?

2. Following the death of her father, Laurel thinks, "I knew nothing will break anymore." What does this mean?

3. Why do you think the author chose the tarot to provide the structural and symbolic underpinnings for her novel? Is this an effective device?

4. Is Laurel a reliable narrator? Does she tell us the truth about her life, or is her narrative view skewed by emotional disorder or even madness?

5. Is Jack a real person, a creation of Laurel's disturbed imagination, or both? Are there possible connections between Jack and Laurel's late father? Or between these two and the canyon rapist?

6. What is the significance of Jack and Laurel making love in the ruins of the magician Houdini's mansion?

7. What does the recurring figure of the tiger symbolize and how does this change as the narrative progresses?

8. Food is an important symbol in *The Hanged Man*. Why does Laurel refuse to eat, and why is her mother obsessed with cooking? What does this say about the relationship of mother and daughter?

9. Why does the author introduce the character of the child Perdita? Does this character have symbolic value in any way?

10. In what ways has the author been influenced by fairy tale and myth in the creation of this novel?

11. Discuss the importance of art in *The Hanged Man*. How has it figured in the lives of Laurel's parents, and how will it have an impact on her own life?

12. Why does Jack disappear at the end of the book?

FRANCESCA LIA BLOCK, nurtured by a painter/filmmaker father and a poet mother, grew up in Los Angeles in the shadow of Laurel Canyon, a beautiful place of natural magic and ghostly memories. She wrote most of her first novel, *Weetzie Bat*, as a student at the University of California–Berkeley. Since then she has written four Weetzie sequels that—like the first—have received high praise and prestigious awards. The luminous Weetzie Bat books are also available in a single volume, *Dangerous Angels*. Ms. Block also is the author of the novels *The Hanged Man*, *I Was a Teenage Fairy*, *Violet & Claire*, *The Rose and The Beast*, *Echo*, *Wasteland*, the short story collection *Girl Goddess #9: Nine Stories*, and *Guarding the Moon*, her chronicle of motherhood. Francesca Lia Block lives in Los Angeles, California.